First published in 2013 by Child's Play (International) Ltd
Ashworth Road, Bridgemead, Swindon SN5 7YD UK

Published in USA by Child's Play Inc
250 Minot Avenue, Auburn, Maine 04210

Distributed in Australia by Child's Play Australia Pty Ltd
Unit 10/20 Narabang Way, Belrose, NSW 2085

ISBN 978-1-84643-633-8
SJ260123CPL03236338

Printed in Shenzhen, China

5 7 9 10 8 6

A catalogue record of this book
is available from the British Library

www.childs-play.com

THE ACROBAT

ALBOROZO

The acrobat
worked in
a circus.

Nobody ever
noticed him.

They watched
the astounding
Adele.

And Hercule the weightlifter.

And Marguerite the Magnificent.

So the acrobat
decided he would leave.

He came to a park.

He was ready to be noticed.

He juggled.

Nobody noticed.

He tumbled.

Nobody noticed.

He balanced.

Nobody noticed.

He cartwheeled.

Nobody noticed.

He squeezed.

Nobody noticed.

It was no good!

The acrobat
decided to feed
the birds instead.

More birds came.

And people noticed.

And more...and more...

...until...